Elementary
Teacher's Manual
for
A Land Remembered:
Student Edition

by
Tillie Newhart and Lee Powell

Pineapple Press, Inc.
Sarasota, Florida

Elementary
Teacher's Manual
for
A Land Remembered: Student Edition
by Patrick D. Smith

ISBN-10: 1-56164-228-2
ISBN-13: 978-1-56164-228-1

Published by
Pineapple Press, Inc.
P.O. Box 3889
Sarasota, Florida 34230-3889
www.pineapplepress.com

About the cover: An 1890 photograph of Sunnyside School, built by Sam Lupfer, I, superintendent of the Disston Sugar Mills, for the children of the mill's employees. It was located in what is now St. Cloud, Florida. A replica was constructed by the Cannery Museum of Florida History (901 Virginia Ave., St. Cloud, FL 34769).

Table of Contents

Introduction

Patrick Smith's, *A Land Remembered*, is an historical Florida treasure. As fourth grade teachers of Florida history, we have read this book aloud to our students and watched as the book came to life for them. Since we abridged and simplified as we read, we realized that a student edition was needed so young people everywhere might learn about Florida's history in an exciting way. With the permission of Patrick Smith, who created this wonderful story of Florida pioneers, and the help of the staff at the Pineapple Press, it is now available for teachers and children and is sure to become a treasure in their hearts forever.

The book tells the tale of the MacIvey family, headed by Tobias MacIvey who abandoned his Georgia farm in 1858 and loaded up a few possessions in a horse-drawn wagon. Along with his wife and infant son, he headed south into the Florida wilderness in search of a new life. It follows three generations of MacIveys (1858-1968) and tells how they at first eked out a living as poor cattle-hunters and then became wealthy landholders. The novel reveals the hopes and concerns of each new generation. It tells of the friendships with the persecuted blacks and Indians, and their respect for the land and its wildlife. Finally, in the words of author Patrick Smith, it teaches us about "livin', lovin', and dyin'."

In our classes we are concerned about preserving our quickly disappearing heritage and environment. *A Land Remembered* lends itself to an integrated, across-the-curriculum study of Florida—its history, geography, and ecology. From this study, a community-wide project has grown that involves the students in the development of a museum of Florida history. The Cannery Museum is recognized nationally as the only kid-run museum in the country and is located at 901 Virginia Ave., St. Cloud, FL, 34769.

We use the Foxfire approach to learning (see the Foxfire Core Practices, p. 57). As each new group of students works with the project, we see how new ideas and activities spiral from the old. The play, based on *A Land Remembered* (included in this guide), developed as the students identified with the characters. Because of the need to have a place to perform the play the old Cannery building was transformed into a theater.

In your journey through this book, you will find a representation of many of the early cultures that made Florida what it is today. Patrick Smith gives you a true picture of what it was like to be an early cow hunter who relied on the Seminole Indians for help with rounding up the wild cattle left behind by the Spanish conquistadors. Smith also interweaves Florida's role in the Civil War and the plight of African Americans after the war. *A Land Remembered* also gives an accurate and vivid picture of the early days of Florida's cattle industry.

I | Language Arts

Overview of Integrated Learning Activities

- Create Literature Circles and Literature Logs to record vocabulary words, chapter summaries, questions, illustrations, reflections.

- Do vocabulary activities.

- Make a list of slang and translations such as: hankerin'/wishing, afore/before, mite/little, skeeters/mosquitoes, plumb/totally.

- Do dialect matching activity page.

- Answer the multiple choice questions and write the answers to comprehension questions using the FCAT format provided.

- Write poems and songs while listening to nature tapes or CDs.

- Write a play and perform it, or use the copy of the play written by the Cannery Kids.

- Cut out the paper dolls of the characters and create stick puppets or a storyboard to retell the story.

- Use the coloring pages to spur class discussions about what was read.

1 | Creating a Literature Log

Students need time to respond to a book in order to make it more meaningful. Small groups of students may form literature circles to read and discuss each chapter of the book. Before they begin reading, students will set up a literature log in a notebook or three-pronged folder in which different reading activities will be recorded. They can illustrate the cover of the folder or create a cover page for their notebook. Have students copy the table of contents from the board. Have students use the table of contents as a checklist of activities to be completed.

Table of Contents Checklist

· Create a list of five comprehension questions each time you read. Discuss these questions in your group.
· Create a character web of each main character.
· Write and illustrate a summary of each chapter.
· Complete the graphic organizer.
· Write the meanings of vocabulary words.
· Complete the story map (see example).
· Research — Florida — see list of topics.
· Complete the — What Did You Think About it? — Worksheet (see example).
· Other things that can be added to the table of contents:

Create murals — dioramas — roller TV shows — pictures — paintings
Papier-mâché — sculpture — mobiles — posters — design a book jacket
or
Students can perform dramatized versions of the literature or create a puppet show.

What Did You Think About It?
Worksheet

1. Do any of the characters remind you of someone you know? Explain.

2. If you had written the story, what changes might you have made in it?

3. Have you ever felt like one of the characters in the story? Explain.

4. Think about how a character solved a problem in the story. Did you learn something from this solution that could be of use to you when you have a similar problem? Explain.

5. If the characters in the story were sitting next to you, what would you like to ask them?

6. Did the setting for the story remind you of a place you have been? Explain.

7. Switch places with your favorite character in the story. How would you behave if you were in the story?

2| Expository and Narrative Writing Prompts to Prepare for the *Florida Writes* Test:

Expositories

1. Explain how cattle came to be wild in Florida and how the cow hunters caught them.
2. Why was the marshtackie important to the Florida settlers? Other topics: citrus, catch dog, and whip
3. Sol was sorry that he had destroyed the natural environment in order to build the MacIvey's empire. Explain why it is important to use our natural resources wisely and preserve animal habitats.
4. Explain why and how the Seminole Indians were forced into the Everglades.
5. Explain how the Civil War affected the Florida settlers.
6. Explain how the railroad changed the way of life for the settlers.

Narratives

1. Imagine that you are a child moving with your family into Florida in 1860. Write about the difficulties that you may have faced or exciting adventures you may have had.
2. Tell the story of Indian children who escaped from the "Trail of Tears" and made their way back to Florida. Explain why the Indian people were forced to walk to a reservation in the West.
3. You are a child growing up in the Florida wilderness. Tell a story about your adventures on a cattle drive to Punta Rassa.
4. Your papa has said that you are old enough to have your own marshtackie. Tell of an adventure you and your horse have together in the Florida wilderness.

3 | Vocabulary Activity Ideas

Assign a **Word of the Day** from the vocabulary list and challenge your students to use that specific vocabulary word from the story at least three times in one day.

Play **Vocabulary Concentration**. Divide the class into groups. Have students make two sets of cards the same size and color. On one set have them write the words with a different symbol next to each word. On the second set have them write the definitions with the matching symbol from the word card. All cards are mixed together and placed face down on a table. A player picks two cards. If the pair matches the word with its definition, the player keeps the cards and takes another turn. If they don't match, they are returned to their places face down, and another player takes a turn. The game is over when all matches have been made.

Play **Vocabulary Charades**. In this game, vocabulary words are acted out and the class must guess what the word is.

Play **20 Clues** with the whole class. In this game, one student selects a word and gives clues about this word, one by one, until someone in the class can guess the word.

As a group activity, have students work together to create an **Illustrated Dictionary** of the vocabulary words.

Play **True or False**. Divide the class into two teams. Write the words on index cards. A word is drawn from a hat, box, or bag by one team. A player on the other team must then give a definition. It can either be true or false. Then a player on the other team must decide if it's true or false. If correctly guessed, the team gets a point. The team with the most points wins.

4 | Dialect Activity

Florida Cracker Cowhunter Dialect

Draw a line to match each word with its meaning

1.	hankerin'	a.	harmful animals
2.	afore	b.	mosquitoes
3.	mite	c.	animals
4.	skeeters	d.	wishing
5.	plumb	e.	all the way
6.	critters	f.	before
7.	vittles	g.	haven't eaten
8.	varmints	h.	little
9.	shinny	i.	out of
10.	bushwhack	j.	climb
11.	ain't et	k.	food
12.	outen	l.	attack

5 | Coloring Pages

Letter from the Artist

The drawings you will find on these pages represent things that would have been common in the days of *A Land Remembered*. The Florida red wolf is now extinct. At one time hundreds of them could be seen along the Oklawaha River. The Army issue McClellan saddle is drawn from one that was already an antique the day my husband's grandfather gave it to him when he was a boy.

The little Florida scrub jay is native to the scrub. This endangered bird is found nowhere else in the United States. It is dove gray underneath. The head, wings and tail are azure blue. The throat is white with a blue band below. The sandhill crane is all gray except for red feathers at the top of the head above the eye.

The cracker house and chickee hut would have been familiar sights to Zech and his family. Just imagine them about to step out into the Florida sunshine as they go about their daily lives almost 150 years ago. I hope you enjoy these drawings as you explore your Florida heritage.

—Regina Stahl Briskey

Sandhill Crane

Cracker Horse

Wild Hog

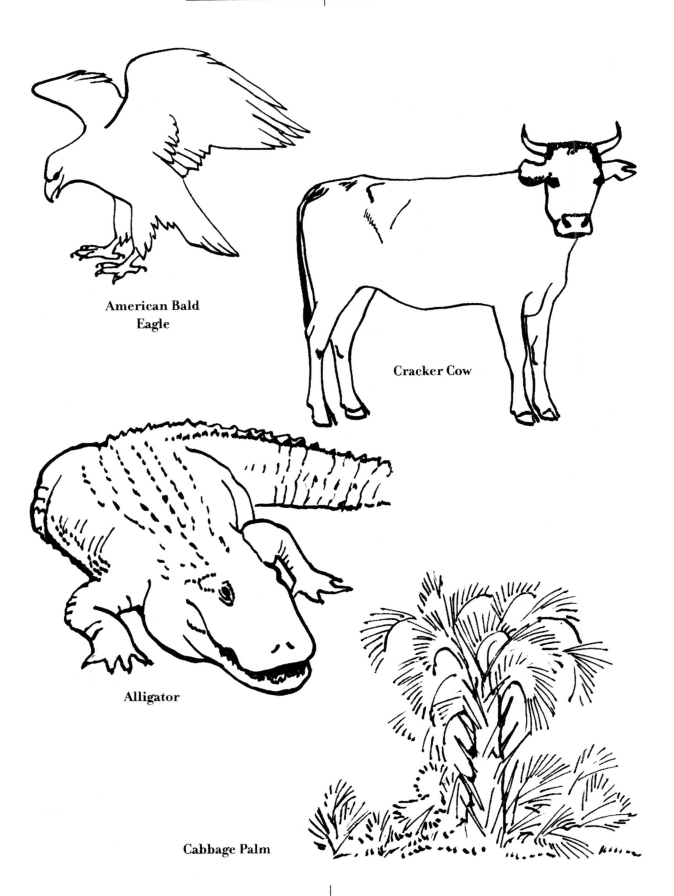

**American Bald
Eagle**

Cracker Cow

Alligator

Cabbage Palm

Florida Turkey

Florida Black Bear

McClellan Saddle

Florida Scrub Jay

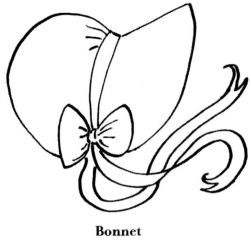

Bonnet

Cracker House

Chickee Hut

Wolf

6| The Play—A Land Remembered
A novel by Patrick Smith
Play written by the Cannery Kids

Emma
Tell you about those early Florida years?
I'll tell you, child, how it was.
When Tobias said, "Let's go,"
I packed up that horse drawn wagon.
I loaded up my baby, Zech,
And we started out through the wilderness.

We came south out of Georgia in 1858—
A sack of corn and a sack of sweet potatoes,
A shotgun and a few shells,
A few dishes and forks and a cast-iron pot.
We brought the tools we would need
To clear the land and build a house.

Tobias
I was so frightened when I returned
From the battle.
The house was gone.
They were our own men
Who burned our home,
Confederate deserters.
"We'll leave this place and go south to the Wilder-
    ness."

My boy Zech, boy and horse,
One and the same.
One night in the scrub
A man-child killed a bear
With a shotgun weighing as much as he.

Zech
That stallion appeared in our corral.
We named him Ishmael.
He was a marshtackie.
Nip and Tuck, the wolf dogs, came too—
A gift from the Seminoles.

Keith Tiger
You must eat first.
It is the custom of our people.

Dip your spoon into our pot.
The sofkee is good.
The Seminole is your friend, Tobias.

Skillet
My name is Skillet.
I was a slave.
The Civil War made me free.
The MacIveys adopted me as part of their family
    and let me have their last name.
I could wrestle a mule or an alligator.
I took on a gator and lost my britches.

Zech
The storm came, blinding rain and lightning.
The cattle drowned and became buzzard meat.
The family was saved by an Indian mound.
They found protection there.

Tobias
Frog and Bonzo—
Two skinny drovers—
Found them on the streets of Kissimmee.
Brought them home to the ranch.
They will help us get those cows to Punta Rassa.

Frog
We were so hungry when Tobias found us
We ate the whole block of cheese he gave us.
Ms. Emma's vittles just saved our lives.

Bonzo
We worked hard to hunt those cattle
Out of the Florida swamps.
The MacIveys became like family to us.

Tawanda
Zech came to our Seminole camp with his father.
Tobias was very ill with malaria.
Our medicine man saved his life.
I took Zech to see Pay-Hay-Okee—

The River of Grass.
I fell in love with Zech.

Glenda
My daddy was the storekeeper at Ft. Drum.
I met Zech at a Frolic.
There was fiddles and dancing.
We fell in love that night and I later became his
    wife.

Scene One

Frog:
Ain't nothin' but a fool makes his living rubbin' his
    bottom against a saddle all day. Sometimes mine
    feels like it's busted. What you got left in the way
    of grub?

Zech:
Nothin' but a couple of strips of beef and a few
    biscuits.

Bonzo:
Don't even have that, just one scrap of meat that
    looks like it ought to be buried.

Zech:
You want me to kill a rabbit? If you do, I best see to
    it now before it gets dark.

Frog:
What I miss most out here is Miss Emma's vittles. I
    ain't got nothin' left. We ought to have brought
    more supplies or turned around two days ago

Zech:
Pappa said we're not coming back after this. We're
    headin' out for grazin' and besides that, none of
    these cows is marked yet. Frog, you and Bonzo'll
    get credit for all of them.

Frog:
Maybe so—but that don't help my belly none. I'd as
    soon have a big bowl of Miz Emma's hot stew just
    now as the sixty dollars over yonder in the pen. I
    done et enough rabbit my ears is beginning to
    grow (scratches head). I got a good idea. We

couldn't be over a hour's ride from Ft. Drum,
    maybe less. We could go over there and get some
    fresh grub and be back here not long after dark.

Zech:
What about the cows? We can't go off and leave
    them unguarded.

Bonzo:
They ain't goin' nowhere inside that pen. I ain't
    seen no wolf sign in three days. We could leave
    the dogs tied to the fence to watch after them.

Zech:
That'd be like using Nip and Tuck for fish bait.
    Some bears or other varmints come in here, the
    dogs wouldn't have a chance tied to a rail. We'd
    have to take them with us.

Frog:
Ain't nothin' gonna' happen to the cows. We can
    build a fire on both sides of the corral. That
    would keep off anything that comes around till
    we get back.

Zech:
You two go on and I'll stay. I'm not hungry anyway.
    I can make do on what I got.

Bonzo:
We ain't about to leave you out here alone. If some-
    thing happened to you while we're gone, your
    Pap would be really mad. Either you go or
    nobody goes.

Zech: (angrily)
You think I can't handle things by myself.

Frog:
It ain't that and you know it. There's no use in
    getting riled up. Your Pappa wouldn't want
    nobody left alone at night on the prairie—not
    you or me or Bonzo. We gonna' go or not? If we
    ain't, then you might as well shoot that rabbit.

Zech:

Well, if your belly's in that bad ashape, I guess I'll go. But I don't like it. I've seen what can happen to a cow at night, and you have too.

Bonzo:

Ain't nothin' gonna' happen (spoken slowly and deliberately).

Scene Two

Zech:

There was a frolic in Ft. Drum that night. Fiddles and dancin'. It was there I met Glenda. Beautiful hair and white skin not burned brown by the Florida's sun.

Glenda:

I've never seen you here before. My daddy owns that store and usually knows everybody who comes to the frolic. My name's Glenda Turner. What's yours?

Zech:

Zech, Zech MacIvey. We came in for food. We've got cows penned out on the prairie.

Glenda:

You live nearby?

Zech:

Up on the Kissimmee, about a day's ride from here. We're in the cattle business and we're finishing the spring roundup.

Glenda:

You want to dance the next one with me?

Zech:

I don't know how, I've never been to a frolic before.

Glenda:

That's too bad. Would you like some punch? I helped my mother make it and I know it's good. The bowl is on the table at the end of the porch.

Zech:

That would be fine.

Scene Three

Zech:

Did you hear something, Pappa? It could be the wind in the trees.

Tobias:

It was a tinkling sound that caught our ear. It was the keeper of the graves. I stared—unbelieving, then believing. He was a man beyond age. So old that his skin was cracked like alligator hide. He wore only a girdle of brass bells. His body stained red.

Timucuan:

I am a Timucuan. The last of my people. I am the keeper of the graves. Soon I will join the others. I have lived beyond my time. Do not bring your cows into the swamp. In here there is only death. Go back the way you came. This is a burial ground for all who enter.

Tobias:

We did not heed his word. Zech could have died there. Violence came from everywhere—without warning—tails slashing, jaws popping. . . . Gators! Turn back! Turn back! Zech, run to save Tuck.

Scene Four

Zech:

I visited the great marsh Pay-Hay-Okee, the River of Grass. There I met Tawanda Cypress, a beautiful Seminole girl.

Tawanda:

I took Zech to see the Pay-Hay-Okee, River of Grass. We rode in the dugout canoe. Sawgrass stretched into infinity broken only by small island hammocks of hardwood trees and cabbage palms. Pay-Hay-Okee goes to the sea in the south. It is many days' journey to the end. It is very difficult pushing the canoe through the sawgrass. Sometimes the grass is taller than two men. I loved Zech. His father Tobias was kind to my people. They brought us cattle. Our medicine man helped Tobias when he had malaria. Our families were linked together.

Scene Five

Emma:
Tobias MacIvey! You put on that suit! If you don't I'll never cook another bite of food as long as I live.

Tobias:
Well, now. That would be bad, wouldn't it? Well, I guess I'll have to learn how to make stew.

Frog:
For goodness sakes, Mistuh MacIvey, put it on! You heard what Miz Emma said, you want us all to suffer because you're so stubborn?

Skillet:
I'll hold him down and you jerk off them overalls. Then we'll hang him by his feet in a tree, like a hawg at scrapin' time and dress him up real purty.

Tobias:
All right! All right! I'll do it this once, but l still don't know why a man's got to dress up like a circus clown to go to a wedding. Back off now! I can do it by myself.

Emma:
That's better. Let's get ready for Zech and Glenda's wedding.

Scene Six

Zech:
Solomon MacIvey was born March 12, 1883. Stamped from his father's mold. A MacIvey through and through; a natural one on a horse. He could ride like the wind.

Emma:
Glenda loved the Kissimmee wilderness. She taught Zech and Sol to read.

(Zech, Emma, and Glenda leave the stage)

Sol: (As an old man)
Where did it all go, Pappa? They were all out there (in a faraway voice, as if way off in the past with them)—the MacIveys all . . . burned brown by prairie sun and wind. Livin', lovin', dyin'. Emma cooking up her vittles . . . Zech galloping wildly on a marshtackie . . . Skillet throwing a bull with just a twist of his powerful body . . . Frog and Bonzo stuffing themselves with hot stew as Emma put more bowls on the table . . . Glenda in her boots and jeans . . . Tobias, looking like a living scarecrow in his faded overalls and wide-brimmed hat, leading all of them westward toward Punta Rassa. . . .
Where did it all go, Pappa?
Where did it all go?

7 | Paper Dolls of the Characters

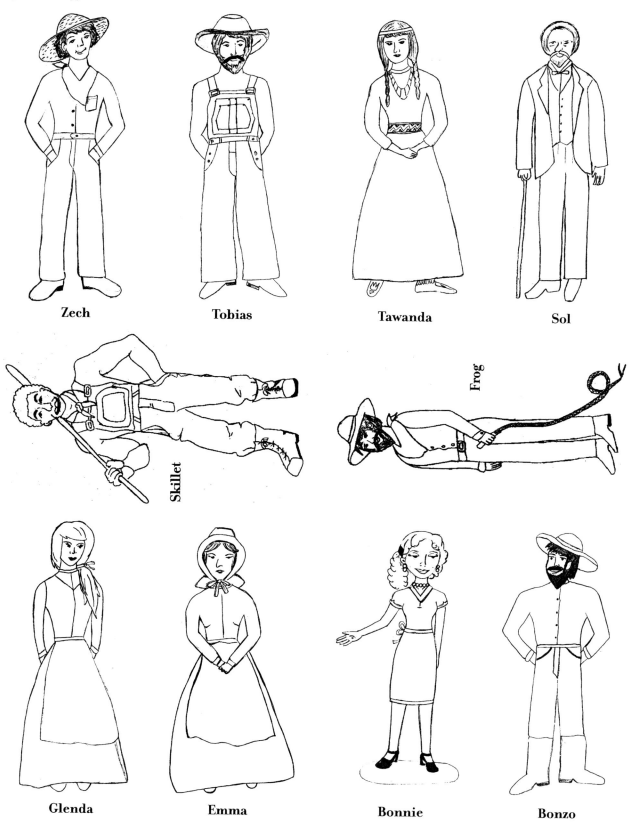

Zech Tobias Tawanda Sol

Skillet Frog

Glenda Emma Bonnie Bonzo

8 | Comprehension Questions for the Literature Log

Chapters 1-6

1. Why did Tobias and Emma leave Georgia in 1858 and move south into the Florida wilderness?

2. Describe how they built their house. How long did it take?

3. Why was it so hard for Tobias to grow a vegetable garden?

4. What did Jenkins, the shopkeeper, hide under a plank in his floor from the rebel army? Why did he hide these things?

5. Describe the strange behavior of the Carolina parakeets that Tobias said caused them to be wiped out in Georgia.

6. What kind of bull did Tobias and Zech kill in the rye meadow?

7. Tobias and Emma could use every part of the bull that Tobias killed. Name two parts of the bull and how they would be used by Tobias and Emma.

8. Explain how Zech and Emma defended their homestead from the bears.

9. Addler tells Tobias that the rebel army needs cattle drovers more than it needs soldiers. Why do you think the rebel army would need cattle drovers more than soldiers?

10. What happened while Tobias was away cutting logs for the rebel army that made him decide to move further south? How do you think he felt when he decided to move away from his homestead? Explain.

Answer Key to Comprehension Questions for Chapters 1–6

1. Tobias had failed at farming in Georgia. They were seeking a new life in an unknown land. Also, the coming Civil War had already been felt in Georgia. Tobias thought the war would not affect Florida as it would Georgia and he would be left alone.

2. More than a year went into completing the log structure. He cut the logs and drug them to the site with the oxen. He shaped the logs and lumber by hand. The roof was made of cypress shingles. He made twenty-five a day. It took more than five hundred to complete the roof. He still had to build the furniture.

3. It was hard to grow a vegetable garden because the soil was poor and the wild animals kept eating it because he didn't have a fence to keep them out.

4. Jenkins hid some powder and shot under a loose plank of the floor. He knew that people would be in trouble without ammunition for protection. They also needed it to kill wild game for food.

5. If one Carolina Parakeet was shot, the others would come back to it — maybe to grieve over the dead. The hunters realized they could kill every one of them this way. Their feathers were used to decorate ladies' hats.

6. It was an Andalusian bull. The bull was bluish-roan in color with huge horns spanning three feet each.

7. Every ounce was used. The tail was chopped into sections for stew. The leg bones and ribs would go into soup. Brains would be scooped out and fried. The hooves would be boiled into jelly. The hide and the horns would be sold.

8. First, they lit torches to try to scare them away with fire. Then they opened the smokehouse so the bears would eat the meat and leave the oxen in the barn alone. When Emma got trapped by one of the bears, Zech drug the shotgun from the house and shot it. The load of shot hit the bear with such force it knocked him into the wall of the woodshed ten feet away. They both made it safely back to the house. The other bear ate the meat in the smokehouse and ran away, leaving Tuck and Buck alone.

9. The army would need cattle drovers more because the soldiers had to be fed and the wild cattle could be rounded up and driven to the Georgia border.

10. When Tobias returned from cutting logs he found his homestead in ashes. It was all burned down by fifteen Confederate deserters. They also killed and ate one of his oxen and took the other one with them. Tobias was angry and he said, "We'll go south. This time we'll go to a place where nobody can find us until the war is over."

9 | Comprehension Questions Using FCAT Format – Ten Lessons

EXERCISES USING EXCERPTS FROM *A LAND REMEMBERED*

DIRECTIONS:
- Each of these exercises has been formulated for the FCAT (Florida Comprehension Assessment Test) for Reading.
- The FCAT has three types of questions: Multiple Choice, Short Response, and Extended Response.
- Read the paragraphs that have been taken from *A Land Remembered*. Think about what you already know from the book and about the excerpt you just read. Answer the questions.

EXCERPT 1: After a Civil War battle, Tobias finds a dead Union soldier in the woods.

At one point the advancing soldiers overran each other and formed one big mass of slashing swords and firing guns. It was impossible to tell one army from the other except for the color of uniforms. As he watched the battle intensify, Tobias wondered what would have happened if they were all dressed in overalls as he was.

The battle raged back and forth for four hours, and then the Federal troops turned and retreated rapidly back to the east. Confederates swooped after them, rushing over a plain now littered with bodies, lifeless men in both blue and gray.

Tobias turned and went back into the woods. He headed south alone. He had walked just over a mile when he cut around a canebrake and found the horse. It was tied to a bush, and the rider was lying on the ground, wearing a blood-soaked blue uniform.

He was a boy of no more than eighteen. Lead balls had caught him in the neck and chest, and Tobias wondered how he could have ridden this far from the battle before falling.

Tobias removed a pistol and scabbard from the soldier's side, and then he unfastened the ammunition belt and put it in one saddlebag. There was also a rifle strapped to the saddle. He said, "I might as well take all of this, fellow, but I want you to understand I ain't stealing from the dead. It ain't no use to you any more, and it will be a godsend for me out in the scrub. I won't bury you, cause they'll find you sooner or later and send you back home. And I know you'd rather be with your folks than here in these woods."

He then searched the other saddlebag and found a knife and several tins of beef. He opened one can and ate ravenously, washing it down with water from the soldier's canteen. Then he mounted the horse and rode south.

(Excerpt from Volume I, Chapter Six)

Multiple Choice Questions:

1. The Civil War battle lasted for
   a. thirty minutes
   b. a week
   c. four hours
   d. four days

2. Tobias escaped the cannon fire of the battle by
   a. hiding in a cave
   b. running into the woods
   c. climbing a tree
   d. hiding in a creek under the lily pads

3. Tobias could tell one army from the other by
   a. the size of their cannon
   b. their flags
   c. the color of their uniforms
   d. their overalls

4. Tobias found the horse
   a. running through the woods
   b. eating grass
   c. tied to a bush
   d. drinking water from a creek

5. In the saddlebags, Tobias found
    a. a blanket and pillow
    b. ammunition
    c. a knife and tins of beef
    d. a pistol

6a. How would the soldier's gear help Tobias' family survive in the wilderness?

6b. Do you think Tobias made the right decision when he took the soldier's horse, food, and equipment? Explain why he should have taken the things, or why he should have left them.

EXCERPT 2: Tobias meets Keith Tiger, Bird Jumper, and Lilly at a Ft. Pierce camp.

Tobias started a fire and then sat by it, eating the last small scrap of coon meat. He had heard no sound of footsteps, but when he glanced to the far reaches of the fire's light, he saw two men and a woman standing there, looking at him. He jumped backward quickly and grabbed the rifle.

One of the men said, "We did not mean to frighten you. We saw your fire and came to it. We mean no harm."

As they came closer, Tobias recognized them as Indians. He said, "I know you. I don't remember the names, but you came to my place in the scrub when the men were chasing you for killing a calf."

"We remember you well," one of the men said. "You are Tobias MacIvey. We have never forgotten what you did for us, and all of our people know of this. But we never expected to find you here. Do you not still live where you did?"

"No. Some men burned the place while I was away, and we left after that. We live now in a hammock on the east bank of the Kissimmee, about a day's journey from here. I'm sorry, but I have no food to offer you now."

"We have food. We will prepare it here if we can share your fire."

"You are welcome," Tobias said. "And you can stay the night if you wish. It would be better for all of us to be together. I've been told there are many strangers wandering the countryside."

One of the men went into the darkness and returned pulling a sled made of two poles covered with deer hide. Several bundles were on the sled.

The men sat with Tobias by the fire as the woman took a pot from the sled and filled it from a deer hide pouch. Then she poured water into the pot and set it on the fire.

"It is sofkee," Keith Tiger said, noticing Tobias' curiosity as he watched Lillie. "We make it by soaking crushed corn in wood ash lye. Then we boil it with water. It is a favorite of our people. When it is done you will eat with us.

"We are on our way to Fort Capron for bullets. The man who owns the trading post at Fort Dallas will not sell guns or bullets to an Indian, and we have heard that the man here will. We need them badly to kill game, and we are on the way to trade for them."

"I had coon skins," Tobias said, "and all I could get for them was salt. For everything else he wanted cash. What do you have to trade?"

"Flour."

"Flour?" Tobias questioned, his interest aroused immediately. "You've got flour?"

"Yes," Keith Tiger responded, amused by Tobias' reaction. "Koonti flour. It is as good as the white man's flour. We like it better. It is made from the root of the Sago palm, and it is free for the taking."

"I've never heard of it, but I reckon I've eaten a ton of cattail flour."

"This is better. We will tell you how to gather it and how to prepare it. In hard times, koonti will nourish you and keep you alive. It saved my people from hunger many times during the wars."

"I'd be right pleased to know all about it," Tobias said. "And the man at the trading post did say he can sell anything a man can eat. You ought to make a good trade."

Keith Tiger motioned toward the sled; then the woman went to it and removed one of the bundles. As she handed it to Tobias, Tiger said, "Take some of the koonti with you. We have enough to share. Tell your woman to use it as she would the white man's flour."

"I really appreciate this,"' Tobias said, accepting the bundle. "I'll have my wife make biscuits as soon as I get back home. And I have something to share too, just in case things go wrong at the trading post." He removed two boxes of the shells from his saddlebag and handed them to Tiger. The Indian's eyes flashed pleasure and gratitude. "This is truly a great gift to my people," he said.

"We will use them wisely, and we do thank you."
(Excerpt from Volume I, Chapter Eight)

Multiple Choice Questions:
1. The Indians carried their food
   a. in their saddlebags
   b. in their backpacks
   c. on a sled made of two poles and deer hide
   d. they had no food
2. The Indians made sofkee out of
   a. mashed potatoes
   b. wild bananas
   c. crushed corn
   d. sour oranges
3. Koonti flour is made from
   a. Sago Palm root
   b. sugarcane
   c. grape vine
   d. cattails
4. Lillie Tiger carried water in a
   a. gourd
   b. canteen
   c. deer hide pouch
   d. clay jug
5. Tobias gave the Indians a gift of
   a. salt
   b. a milk cow
   c. a marshtackie
   d. two boxes of shells

6a. How did Tobias know the three Indians who appeared at his camp?

6b. Explain why the Indians were friendly and how they helped Tobias.

EXCERPT 3: Frog and Bonzo, Two Skinny Drovers

Emma asked Tobias, "Why don't you find some help driving the cattle? There must be a lot of homeless men somewhere who need work. You could try to get help up at Kissimmee."

Tobias said, "I'll go to Kissimmee at daybreak tomorrow."

Tobias approached Kissimmee along a dirt road deeply embedded by cows' hooves. He first rode all the way through town. He came to a store, dismounted, tied his horse to a rail, and walked back to a skinny man with a bushy, black beard. He asked bluntly, "You lookin' for work?"

The man glanced up. "Doing what?"

"Brush popping."

"What's that?"

"Working cows. Herding. You want the job or not? I'm riding out of here just as soon as I can. I'm Tobias MacIvey. What's your name?"

"Frog."

"Frog? Frog what?"

"Just Frog. That's all the name I need. I got a buddy down the street. Can he go too?"

"Yes. I need two drovers. What's his name?"

"Bonzo."

Tobias shook his head. "Frog and Bonzo. This is going to be some cattle crew. Go and tell him we'll leave from right here in a half hour. And both of you better be on time."

Tobias went into the store and said to the clerk, "Can you make a sign?"

"What do you want it to say? Why don't you write down for me what you want it to say and I'll copy it."

"If I could write it down, I'd make the sign myself. I ain't no good at writing and reading. That's what I'm paying you for."

Frog and Bonzo were standing in the street when Tobias came out of the store.

Tobias said, "We got some riding to do afore dark."

(Excerpt from Volume I, Chapter Fourteen)

Multiple Choice Questions:

1. Frog and Bonzo were
   a. Zech's favorite dogs
   b. two homeless cowboys
   c. the oxen
   d. two Indian boys

2. The town of Kissimmee
   a. had a dirt trail for cattle
   b. was a port city
   c. was a large rail depot
   d. had a casino

3. Brush popping is
   a. picking berries
   b. buck dancing
   c. cow herding
   d. alligator shooting

4. Tobias hired Frog and Bonzo
   a. for protection
   b. to drive cattle
   c. because he was lonely
   d. to be cooks

5. Tobias needed the storekeeper to make his sign because he
   a. was in a hurry
   b. didn't have paint
   c. needed shoes to put on his horse
   d. couldn't read or write

6a. Why did Tobias need to hire Frog and Bonzo?

6b. Tobias couldn't write what he needed on the sign. How do you think he felt about that? Explain your answer.

EXCERPT 4: The Timucuan in the swamp.

When Tobias got back to the wagon, Emma asked, "Well, did you see any buggers out there tonight?"

"No, but I swear, Emma, I heard bells. Zech heard it too, and I told him it was just the wind in the trees. But it wasn't. It was bells."

Tobias was a mile into the dark and gloomy swamp when he heard it, the bells, the one thing he had come looking for—not a passage for the herd but the strange sound that had come out of the night. It was off to the right, no more than a hundred yards distant, tinkling, moving and then stopping, then moving again. He sat in his saddle, not thinking of the herd or anything but the bells.

The horse whinnied and backed away a few steps as the sound grew louder, then it came past the last clump of palmetto and stood before him.

The man was beyond age, so old that his skin was cracked like alligator hide. He was almost seven feet tall, and his hair was tied on top of his head with bands of reeds, making him seem even taller. He word only a girdle of silver-colored balls and small brass bells, and around his neck there were six strings of shells. His wrists were covered with bracelets of fish teeth, and his entire body was stained red.

For several moments no word was spoken, and then the old man said, "I am a Timucuan, the last of my people. I am the keeper of the graves. Soon I will join the others. We came here a long time ago to hide from the Spanish soldiers. I am the only one left, and I have lived beyond my time."

Tobias said, "We didn't know. We are lost and trying to find a passage for the herd."

"Do not bring your cows in here," the old man cautioned. "In here there is only death. If you come in here you will never return. Go back the way you came. This swamp is a burial ground for all who enter. My people have known this to be true. Only death awaits you if you enter."

Without speaking further, the old man turned and walked away.

Zech rode to Tobias swiftly as soon as he emerged from the woods. He asked anxiously, "Did you find it, Pappa?"

"Find what?"

"The bells, Pappa, did you find the bells?"

"It was the wind. Only the wind. Ride on ahead and tell the men to move the cows out of here right away. Hurry now!"

(Excerpt from Volume I, Chapter Fifteen)

Multiple Choice Questions:
1. The swamp
    a. was a cool place for swimming
    b. had a saltwater pond
    c. was dark and gloomy
    d. was covered with red flowers
2. The Timucuan told Tobias that the swamp was
    a. good grazing
    b. the burial ground for all who entered
    c. a good place for fishing
    d. filled with animals for hunting
3. The Timucuan was
    a. hiding from soldiers
    b. chief of his people
    c. keeper of the graves
    d. happy to meet Tobias
4. The Timucuan was wearing
    a. bracelets of fish teeth
    b. six strings of shells around his neck
    c. a girdle of silver-colored balls and small brass bells
    d. all of the above
5. The Timucuan's entire body was stained
    a. blue
    b. black
    c. red
    d. yellow

6a. Describe the Timucuan.

6b. Why didn't Tobias tell Zech about the Timucuan with the bells? Explain.

EXCERPT 5: Cattle Drive to Punta Rassa for Shipment to Cuba

❝How would you like to see a place called Punta Rassa?"

"Where's that?" Zech asked.

"Over on the west coast, clear across the state, on the Gulf of Mexico. They're buying cows there now for Cuba at twelve dollars a head. As soon as our cows hit five hundred pounds each we're heading west. I figure it ought to be more than three weeks, maybe less.

The line of cattle stretched nearly a quarter of a mile, moving slowly. The men and dogs flanking the sides, the wagon in the rear. Frog told Tobias he had never been to Punta Rassa but knew of men who had, and that they should go south to Fort Basinger where there was a ferry to take the wagon across the Kissimmee River.

The village had a desolate look. Tobias had pictured it differently, the name Punta Rassa conjuring visions of something exotic, things he had never seen before. But except for the cattle dock and more numerous buildings, it was no different from Kissimmee.

Several men were sitting on the porch of one store, and Tobias rode up to them and dismounted. He said, "I'm looking for a cattle buyer. Know where I can find one?"

"Down yonder," one of the men said, pointing. "The shack on the dock. You want to see Cap'n Hendry."

In the dock shack, Tobias said, "Name's Tobias MacIvey. I was told I could find a cattle buyer here."

"You come to the right place," the man said, getting up from the rocker. He was a tall, slim man of about fifty. "I'm Sam Hendry. Where's your herd?"

"Three miles up the river."

"How many you got?"

"Can't say for sure. I figure it to be around eight hundred and fifty."

"They in good shape?"

"Real good. They ought to go over five hundred pounds each."

"That's the kind we need," Hendry said. "Some

27

men run them yellowhammers down here like they was rabbits instead of cows. Time they get here they're not much more than skin and bones. If they're in good shape like you say, we'll pay sixteen dollars a head. If not, twelve is tops. Drive the herd on down here and put them in one of the holding pens. We pay in Spanish gold doubloons worth fifteen dollars each. You'll need to buy a trunk to carry your money."

When they counted the cows, it came to eight hundred sixty-five head, all in good shape, so the price was sixteen. That came to thirteen thousand eight hundred forty dollars.

(Excerpt from Volume I, Chapter Fifteen)

Multiple Choice Questions:
1. Punta Rassa is located on
   a. the Kissimmee River
   b. Miami Beach
   c. the Gulf of Mexico
   d. the Atlantic Ocean
2. Yellowhammers are
   a. yellow-headed woodpeckers
   b. cow dogs
   c. a team of oxen
   d. skinny wild cows
3. A doubloon is a
   a. Spanish uniform
   b. water lily
   c. gold coin
   d. small songbird
4. The top price that the MacIveys received for the cattle sold in Punta Rassa was
   a. a trunk full of gold ($13,840)
   b. forty acres of swampland
   c. a wagonload of cotton
   d. a fine team of oxen
5. The MacIveys reached Punta Rassa with
   a. two herds of cows
   b. one thousand cows
   c. 865 head of cattle
   d. three-dozen yellowhammers

6a. Describe Punta Rassa.

6b. Explain why the MacIveys received top price for the cattle delivered to Punta Rassa.

EXCERPT 6: The Mosquitoes

The rain stopped just before dawn, and daybreak came once again to a cloudless sky. Tobias stirred and said, "We needed rain real bad, but that one was almost too much. I hope nobody floated away."

He got out of the wagon and walked across the soggy ground, stopping at the rim of the basin. The herd was all there, standing in a sheet of water covering the marsh.

Because the basin was low land and mucky rather than sandy, the water did not run off quickly or become absorbed. Instead, it dropped to a one-inch cover and remained that way, releasing millions upon millions of mosquito eggs attached to the grass, dormant eggs that would incubate quickly in the intense heat and turn into larvae. Each invisible larva would eat and breathe for four days, and after shedding its skin four times, become a pupa. At this stage it discontinued eating and changing rapidly, and in another two days its skin split, allowing an adult mosquito to pull itself out and dry its wings in preparation for flight. No one in camp was aware of this natural chain of events taking place across the tranquil marsh.

Tobias and Skillit were with the herd, puzzled by the faint humming sound drifting across the marsh from the north. Then they saw it, a solid black cloud extending from the ground thirty feet upward, moving toward them. As they watched, other clouds formed in the west and in the south.

Before they could turn the horses, the stinging came, setting their bodies on fire. Tobias looked down and his legs were covered solidly by mosquitoes. His horse bolted straight upward and crashed down on its side, struggling and kicking, trying to regain its footing.

Cows were bucking, kicking, and falling all around him as Zech raced across the marsh. As soon as a cow hit the ground mosquitoes swarmed over it and formed a solid mass in its mouth and nose, blocking air from its lungs, causing the cow's eyes to pop out as it tried to bellow but could not do so.

The mosquitoes followed them two miles into the prairie until a brisk east wind blew them back toward the marsh.

Tobias went back to the wagon alone at daybreak, dreading what he might find. When he reached the marsh he saw that he no longer had a herd as such. Cows were scattered across the marsh as far as he could see, and there were many lifeless forms. They counted seventy-three dead cows. It took them two days to bring the herd together again.

(Excerpt from Volume I, Chapter Eighteen)

Multiple Choice Questions:
1. The mosquitoes rose out of the swamp within a matter of days after
    a. a fire
    b. a hurricane
    c. the Indians left
    d. the rainstorm
2. The cows and horses tried to get away from the mosquitoes by
    a. snorting
    b. bolting
    c. bucking
    d. all of the above
3. A good brisk wind carried away the
    a. birds
    b. gnats
    c. mosquitoes
    d. fog
4. When a cow fell to the ground the mosquitoes
    a. formed a mass in its nose and mouth
    b. swarmed over it, covering it
    c. blocked air from its lungs
    d. all of the above
5. The swarm of mosquitoes looked like a
    a. thick white fog
    b. flock of birds
    c. black cloud
    d. rainstorm

6a. Describe the stages in the life of a mosquito.

6b. Explain how the mosquito swarm affected the cows.

EXCERPT 7: The Railroad

One morning the MacIveys could see the railroad in the distance as the sun reflected off shiny steel rails. It was the new line into Tampa. Zech and Frog had come upon a section of it under construction while scouting grazing land, and the foreman contracted with them for delivery of two dressed steers each day for forty dollars per steer. When the lead steer reached the rails they could see smoke boiling up on the horizon, painting a black streak in the sky. Soon afterward a tooting sound broke the silence of the prairie. The cows poured halfway across the rails and stopped.

Tobias shouted, "That fool is going to plow right into them!"

Zech and Frog wheeled their horses and got out of the way as the engine smashed into the herd, its iron cowcatcher scooping up three cows, crushing and killing them instantly. The train then came to a stop a hundred yards down the rails.

Zech looked at the mangled bodies and shouted, "What do you mean, fellow? Can't you see a herd of cows a mile away? If you'd stopped that thing, we'd a' got them out of the way! Who's going to pay us for the cows you killed?"

"File a claim with the headquarters office in Tampa," the engineer said. "But don't try to charge us a hundred dollars each for buzzard bait worth fifteen."

None of them noticed Tobias as he walked on the side of the engine, carrying the shotgun. He aimed at the boiler and pulled both triggers, blowing an eight-inch hole in the steel plate. Steam shot out and hissed loudly, like angry rattlesnakes, spewing a white cloud over the engine.

The engineer jumped from the cabin and came to Zech. "Do you know what the old fool has done?" he shouted. "It'll take us a half day to patch the boiler and get up steam again! Who's going to pay for this?"

"We'll swap out," Zech said, trying hard to be serious. "We'll trade you our dead cows for your hole. That ought to about even things up. We'll see you. And good luck with the patchin'."

Frog rode up to Zech and said, "The old man's

still got fire in his guts, ain't he?"

"Sure seems that way," Zech said. "That breech loader has killed everything but a train engine, and now it's done that too."

(Excerpt from Volume II, Chapter Twenty-nine)

Multiple Choice Questions:

1. The MacIveys were providing meat for the
    a.   hotel in Punta Rassa
    b.   railroad crew
    c.   land agent's office
    d.   soldiers at Fort Dallas
2. A cowcatcher is a
    a.   cowboy
    b.   holding pen
    c.   loading chute
    d.   train engine's grill
3. A breech loader is
    a.   a giant hammer
    b.   part of a train engine
    c.   a shotgun
    d.   a wagon axle
4. The breech loader put a hole in the boiler. A boiler is a
    a.   piece of Indian pottery
    b.   blacksmith's tool
    c.   part of a train engine
    d.   big stew pot
5. The new railroad line was going into
    a.   Ft. Myers
    b.   Tampa
    c.   St. Augustine
    d.   Miami

6a. Why did Tobias shoot the train?

6b. Explain why the exchange of the hole in the train and the dead cows was or was not a good swap.

EXCERPT 8: Sol's Vegetable Farm

The two tracts of land Zech had purchased south of Lake Okeechobee were right in the middle of what was to become the most extensive farmland in south Florida. Sol suspected this when he rode his horse onto the section southeast of the lake and examined the rich soil and the lushness of the vegetation. As he gazed out over the land and then explored it, riding past ponds and sloughs filled with snakes and alligators and turtles, coming to areas of open glades where the shadows of egrets and herons and ibises glided over the sawgrass, his first thought was, "How do you turn a place like this into a farm?"

He hired dredges to gash the earth and drain it, paying with Spanish gold, then the men and saws and machines to rip out the giant bald cypress and the hickory and the oak and the cabbage palm and the palmetto and the cocoplum bushes, pushing mounds of dirt over the sawgrass and the seas of violet-blue pickerelweed. It took more than a year, but he gradually turned hammocks and Everglades into fields stretching as far as the eye could see, soil so black it looked like soot. Then he formed the MacIvey Produce Company and hired workers to plant tomatoes, beans, squash, celery, corn, cucumbers, lettuce, and okra, eventually becoming a supplier of vegetables to the growing cities of Palm Beach, Fort Lauderdale, Miami, Fort Myers, Tampa, and Saint Petersburg, also shipping vast quantities by rail to markets in Chicago, New York, and Boston.

(Excerpt from Volume II, Chapter Thirty-nine)

Multiple Choice Questions:

1. Sol prepared the land for planting vegetables by
   a. killing all the wild animals
   b. spreading chemicals
   c. draining and clearing the trees
   d. flooding the land
2. Sol formed a produce company and hired workers to plant
   a. oranges and grapefruit
   b. tomatoes and other vegetables
   c. figs and pineapples
   d. custard apples
3. The vegetation that was growing before Sol cleared the land was
   a. cypress, cabbage palm, and oak
   b. peach and apple trees
   c. sugarcane and okra
   d. wheat fields
4. Sol decided to use the land for a farm because
   a. the soil was rich
   b. there were no snakes and alligators
   c. there were no ponds or sloughs
   d. nothing was growing there
5. Sol sent the vegetables to
   a. France and Germany
   b. Cuba
   c. Chicago, New York, and Boston
   d. California

6a. Describe how Sol built the vegetable farm.

6b. Explain how Sol's development of the land was both good and bad for Florida.

EXCERPT 9: Rift Between the Brothers—Sol Tells Toby that He Has a Farm in Okeechobee

Toby's eyes flashed surprise. He said, "You mean it is you who is destroying the land? I cannot believe this, Sol. Father would have never put an ax to the custard-apple trees. He loved that place. Why is it you are doing this?"

Sol was shocked by the reaction. He said hesitantly, "Like I said, Toby, I'm turning it into farmland. People in the new cities have to eat, and there's beginning to be more and more of them. I'm growing vegetables in the fields."

"Animals have to eat too, and so do birds, and so do we!" Toby said angrily. "Will your infernal machines not stop until they come here and crush my mother's grave? I hope they never enter this swamp, or go into Pay-Hay-Okee. If they do, you will have destroyed us too, all of us!"

Sol got up and said, "I'm sorry you feel this way, Toby. But it's my land now, and I have the right to do whatever I want with it."

"You are a traitor to the wishes of your father!" Toby snapped.

Sol couldn't take it any longer. He said regretfully, "I'm really sorry you said that, Toby. I've only done what I thought was right, but no matter what a person does, he can't please everybody. Someone will object. I'm sorry."

Then he mounted his horse and rode out of the village.

(Excerpt from Volume II, Chapter Thirty-nine)

Multiple Choice Questions:

1. Toby became angry with his half-brother Sol because he
   a. cleared the forest for a farm
   b. became a trapper
   c. never married
   d. shot his favorite dog
2. Toby wanted to save the land for
   a. animals and birds
   b. the Indian people
   c. future generations
   d. all of the above
3. Sol's father Zech bought the custard-apple forest so that
   a. it could be cleared
   b. no one could ever put an ax to it
   c. he could plant an orange grove
   d. he could trap raccoons
4. Moon vines grew
   a. on pine trees
   b. on custard-apple trees
   c. in Lake Okeechobee
   d. on the dike
5. Sol was able to clear the land by using
   a. slaves
   b. machines
   c. Cuban laborers
   d. cowboys

6a. Was Sol sorry about destroying the land? Explain Sol's feelings about what he did.

6b. Explain why Toby was angry with Sol.

EXCERPT 10: Hurricane of 1928

Sol turned left at Belle Glade and headed for the Okeechobee house, leaving Miami because of advance warnings that a hurricane was approaching from the south. Although two years had passed since the savage 1926 storm, the area had not yet fully recovered, and some of the fields lay fallow and unplanted. Sol and Bonnie drove along the sandy trail leading to the lake. Sol stopped the car, and they both gazed at the strange phenomenon. Bonnie said, "What is it, Sol? Is it insects?"

"No, it's pollen," Sol replied. "It's not a good sign, either. Toby Cypress once told me that when sawgrass pollen boils like that it means a great storm is coming. They flee from the sight of it. Maybe it's just another Indian legend. But it's weird, isn't it?"

As they drove back past the stretch of marsh, pollen boiled even more, looking like millions of swarming gnats. Sol stopped briefly and looked again, saying, "If Toby were here, he'd be cutting out for somewhere else. Next thing you know, an owl will light on our roof and cry out. That's an even worse omen."

By mid-afternoon the area outside the house was covered with brown foam as the lake water reached the yard. Waves on the lake gradually increased, starting at two feet and going to six, crashing over the flat banks and rushing southward; and then it came like tidal waves, ten feet high, wall after wall of wind-driven water, uprooting palms and oaks and anything in its way. It inched up the house's foundation, three feet off the ground, then it touched the porch floor and slushed in beneath the doors.

Bonnie stared with horror as the water covered the floor, an inch at first and then three inches, rising rapidly. She wailed, "Oh my God, Sol! What can we do? The whole lake is coming down on us!"

"Stand on a chair!" Sol shouted above the roar. "It can't come higher than that!"

But it did come higher, lapping the top of the dining room table. Then Sol put a chair on top of the table, and climbed through an opening into the roof rafters, pulling Bonnie after him, the two of them clinging to studs as cypress shingles gave way and sailed off like leaves, exposing them to the pounding rain that made breathing almost impossible.

Sol shuddered with anxiety and clung desperately to Bonnie as he felt the house being jolted from its foundation. He felt himself ripped from Bonnie, splashing down into angry, boiling water. His shouts of "Bonnie! Bonnie!" were heard only by himself.

The Okeechobee hurricane of 1928 changed the face of the land forever. The lake was eventually diked, surrounded by such a high mound of dirt that its waters would never again be seen from ground level. Then drainage canals were cut, drying up the soil until summer winds blew it away, turning the life-giving water away from the Big Cypress Swamp and the Everglades, creating drought in dry seasons when the natural flow from the lake no longer came, and flooding in rainy seasons because the earth could no longer absorb it. It was all done with good intent and faith at the time but nevertheless created a travesty against nature that could never be reversed. The hurricane also caused a bad slump in Florida's economy, contributing to the great depression.

(Excerpt from Volume II, Chapter Forty-two)

Multiple Choice Questions:
1. Fallow means
    a. fast
    b. unused
    c. green
    d. ripe
2. Indian legend states that when sawgrass pollen boils it means
    a. there is a full moon
    b. birds will migrate
    c. a great storm is coming
    d. tomorrow will be sunny
3. An omen is
    a. a warning sign
    b. howling wind
    c. drowning crops
    d. a flood

4.   A dike is a
     a.   canal
     b.   dock
     c.   high earth mound
     d.   fence

5.   The Okeechobee dike did *not* cause
     a.   drought
     b.   the drying up of the Everglades
     c.   flooding
     d.   cattle stampedes

6a. Were Floridians of 1926-28 warned of the approaching hurricanes? How are we warned today?

6b. Explain the effects of the 1928 hurricane on Florida. How did the terrible storm affect the state's ecology and economy?

Answer Key for FCAT-formatted Comprehension Questions

Excerpt 1 (from Vol. I):

1. c
2. b.
3. c.
4. c.
5. c.
6a. Guns and ammunition would help kill wild game for food. They would also be used for protection. The canned beef and canteen helped get Tobias home.
6b. The horse would have died if Tobias had left it tied to a bush. The soldier couldn't use the horse, food, and equipment. These things would help Tobias and his family in the wilderness. They could use the horse to catch the wild cows. The guns and ammunition would help to provide meat.   or

   Tobias should not have taken the horse, guns, ammunition, and food that belonged to the dead Union soldier. It is very wrong to steal things from the dead. The dead man's family probably needed his horse and other things. Everybody was having a hard time during the war.

Excerpt 2 (from Vol. I):

1. c.
2. c.
3. a.
4. c.
5. d.
6a. He recognized them as the people who had come to his homestead in the scrub.
6b. The Indians were friendly because Tobias had rescued them from some men who were chasing them for killing a calf. Tobias fed and comforted them. The Indians helped Tobias by giving him koonti flour. The Indian woman made food for Tobias.

Excerpt 3:

1. b.
2. a.
3. c.
4. b.
5. d.
6a. Tobias was trying to round up wild cattle, brand them, and drive them to a market in Punta Rassa. Zech was helping him, but Zech was just a boy. Tobias went to Kissimmee looking for help to herd cattle.
6b. He admitted that he couldn't read or write and he was embarrassed.

Excerpt 4:

1. c.
2. b.
3. c.
4. d.
5. c.
6a. The Timucuan was so old his skin was cracked like alligator hide. His whole body was painted red. He wore a girdle of bells.
6b. Tobias thought that he may have been imagining the whole incident. It was such a ghostly, eerie meeting; he didn't want to frighten Zech. Tobias knew that the swamp was a very dangerous place and he didn't want Zech to go there.

Excerpt 5:

1. c.
2. d.
3. c.
4. a.
5. c.
6a. Punta Rassa was a small port town on the Gulf Coast. It was a cattle market where the beef was shipped to Cuba. It had dirt streets and cow pens.
6b. The MacIveys drove their cattle very slowly to Punta Rassa. They allowed their cows to stop and graze on the tall grass of the prairies. They stopped at good watering holes. They were not in a hurry to get their cows to market. They took good care of their cows

and fattened them up along the way. They were paid top price because the cows were in such good shape.

Excerpt 6:
1. d.
2. d.
3. c.
4. d.
5. c.
6a. The eggs are laid by the adult female mosquito. When rain comes, the eggs hatch. They feed on blood from animals and people.
6b. The cows were bucking, kicking, and falling. As a cow hit the ground, mosquitoes swarmed over its mouth and nose, blocking air from its lungs. When Tobias went back to the wagon, he found 73 dead cows.

Excerpt 7:
1. b.
2. d.
3. c.
4. c.
5. b.
6a. Tobias was angry because the train had run over and killed some of his cows. The train engineer was not apologetic.
6b. The train engineer said the railroad would pay a small amount for the cows. Tobias knew they would not pay what they were worth. He became angry and shot a hole in the train's boiler so it would not run. It was a good swap for Tobias, but not for the railroad.

Excerpt 8:
1. c.
2. b.
3. a.
4. a.
5. c.
6a. Sol cut down the trees, drained the land, and planted vegetables.
6b. Sol's development of the land was good for Florida because it provided food for the people. It was good for the economy because it made jobs for people.   or
     The development was bad because it destroyed the natural environment and ecology. It destroyed animal habitats and dried up parts of the Everglades. It wiped out the custard-apple forest.

Excerpt 9:
1. a.
2. d.
3. b.
4. b.
5. b.
6a. Sol was not sorry about destroying the land. He said, "I've only done what I thought was right, but no matter what a person does, he can't please everybody."
6b. The break was caused by Sol's destruction of the forest to make a farm. Toby wanted to save the land in its natural form.

Excerpt 10:
1. b.
2. c.
3. a.
4. c.
5. d.
6a. Little or no warning was given then. Today we are warned by radio and T.V. Satellites can see the storms. Planes fly into them.
6b. Many people whose homes and businesses were destroyed just gave up and went back north. It brought on a recession in the economy. The storm caused people to build a dike around Lake Okeechobee. This hurt the ecology because it interrupted the natural flow of water to the Everglades.

10|SUNSHINE STATE STANDARDS

Language Arts Grades 3-5

Strand A:	*Reading*	
Standard 1:	*Using the reading process effectively.*	
Benchmarks:	*LA.A.1.2.1:*	*Table of contents, headings, captions, etc.*
	LA.A.1.2.2:	*Word attack strategies*
	LA.A.1.2.3:	*Vocabulary strategies*
	LA.A.1.2.4:	*Clarifies understanding*
Standard 2:	*Constructing meaning from a wide range of texts.*	
Benchmarks:	*LA.A.2.2.1:*	*Main idea*
	LA.A.2.2.2:	*Author's purpose*
	LA.A.2.2.3:	*Persuade*
	LA.A.2.2.6:	*Fact & Opinion*
	LA.A.2.2.7:	*Comparison & contrast*
	LA.A.2.2.8:	*Reference materials*
Strand B:	*Writing*	
Standard 1:	*Using the writing process effectively*	
Benchmarks:	*LA.B.1.2.1:*	*Pre-writing*
	LA.B.1.2.2:	*Drafts*
	LA.B.1.2.3	*Editing*
Standard 2:	*Communicating ideas and information effectively*	
Benchmarks:	*LA.B.2.2.1*	*Notes, comments*
	LA.B.2.2.5:	*Narratives*
	LA.B.2.2.6:	*Expository*
Strand C:	*Listening, Viewing, and Speaking*	
Standard 1:	*The student uses listening strategies effectively*	
Benchmarks:	*LA.C.1.2.1:*	*Listening*
	LA.C.1.2.2:	*Personal listening preferences*
Standard 2:	*Understanding the power of language.*	
Benchmarks:	*LA.D.2.2.1:*	*Word choices*
	LA.E.1.2.2:	*Plot, conflict, characters*
	LA.E.1.2.3	*Settings, events*
	LA.E.1.2.4:	*Attitudes & values*
	LA.E.2.2.3:	*Compare with own life*
	LA.E.2.2.4:	*Theme*
	LA.E.2.2.5:	*Forms own ideas*

II | Social Studies

Overview of Integrated Learning Activities

- Have the class pretend they are Emma or Tobias and keep a log of their travels into Florida.
  1. On the map of Florida, as it was in 1890 (see p. 40), show how they traveled and where their two different homesteads were established.
  2. Add the routes they took on the cattle drives to Punta Rassa, and label Kissimmee, St. Cloud, the Everglades, the Custard-Apple Forest, Miami Beach, and the general area that Sol and Bonnie lived near Lake Okeechobee.
  3. Write about the hardships they faced on a day-to-day basis.
- Record references in their log to the Civil War and how they felt about the war.
- Connect Art to Social Studies by having students create relief maps of Florida using clay (or use recipe for making salt dough) or create a Florida map and use yarn to outline it.
- *A Land Remembered* lends itself to many research topics related to Florida history, geography, and ecology.

1| Map Activities

Relief Maps

A relief map is a small-scale representation of a region. It is special because it shows the physical features of an area. These features may be represented by means of shading, contour lines, and colors on a two-dimensional surface. Land features can be shown in three-dimensional form by using clay or other materials to represent them.

First decide how big your map will be. Using a sturdy piece of cardboard as your base, pencil in an outline of your state. Next, make the dough you will use to show the contours of the land. Use the following materials and directions to help you complete your relief map.

Materials you will need:

Flour

Salt

Water

Bowl

Putty knife

Cardboard or poster board

Newspaper

Directions:

Use your hands to mix 2 parts flour to 1 part salt in a bowl. Slowly add small amounts of water to mixture until it resembles cookie dough. (Keep it stiff enough to make land features.)

Cut the piece of cardboard or poster board the size you wish to make your relief map. Use newspaper under the map to catch any falling dough. Outline your map features on the cardboard or poster board and work the dough into the features you wish to show.

Before the dough hardens, use a putty knife or a table knife to make any main rivers or land features you wish to include. Your relief map should dry overnight, depending on the amount of moisture in the air. On the following day, you can paint your rivers, lakes, hills, forests, and/or whatever else you wish to add.

Soft Dough Clay

1-1/2 cups salt

1 cup water

4 cups flour

1/2 cup cooking oil

1 teaspoon alum

food coloring, as desired

Mix dry ingredients in plastic bowl. Add oil and water gradually. Knead in food coloring. Clay will not harden or sour.

2 | Research Topics

1. The Civil War
2. Endangered Animals of Florida
3. The Seminole Indians
4. Florida Railroads
5. The Use of Steamboats
6. The Everglades
7. Famous Floridians

3 | Gathering Oral History

Objective: Students will seek out and interview the oldest people they can find and ask them about the changes that have taken place during their lifetime.

Have students develop a questionnaire. Some sample questions are:

1. Were you born before
   plastics?
   ballpoint pens?
   credit cards?
   copy machines?
2. What was it like when you were my age?
3. What did you do to help your family?
4. Were there any fast-food restaurants?
5. What did you do for fun?
6. Did you really walk two miles, uphill, through the snow to school every day?

After gathering all the information by taking notes or using a tape recorder, have students either write a story, or present their findings orally to the class.

or

Create an interview poster with illustrations, pictures, and photographs.

4 | **Building a Seminole Home or Chickee Hut**

1. Gather 4 sturdy posts of the same length.
2. Nail and glue flat pieces of wood (sideboards and endboards) to the posts to create a frame (1).
3. Fasten 4 kneebraces to posts and sideboards (2).
4. Nail 3 crossplates on top of the sideboards. Offset the middle crossplate (2).
5. Nail 4 kneebraces to endboards and posts (2).
6. Nail and glue 3 sets of rafters together (3).
7. Nail roof battens to rafters (3 to each side). The middle rafter should be centered so it sits in front of the offset middle crossplate (4).
8. Attach roof assembly to frame by nailing rafters to crossplates.
9. Thatch roof with woven palmetto fronds (5).

1 |
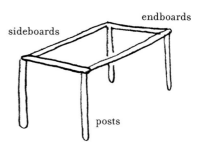

sideboards endboards posts

2 |
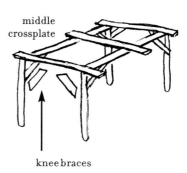

middle crossplate knee braces

3 |
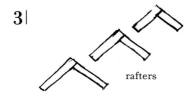

rafters

4 |

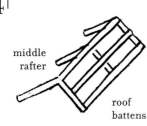

middle rafter roof battens

5 |

The Seminoles had many different kinds of chickees. The "sleeping chickee" had a raised floor for protection from snakes and other wild creatures. Woven mats on the sides were lowered for privacy.

The "cooking chickee" had the traditional fire representing the circle of life.

5 | **Making a Paper Quilt**

Start with a large piece of butcher block paper. Give each student a piece that has been squared off (uniform in size). Measure the big piece to fit the individual drawings.

Plan your border – Seminole patchwork designs make a great border (see samples on p. 45).

Ideas for the theme:
>   Drawings of the characters
>   Events in Florida history
>   Florida symbols
>   5 flags that have flown over Florida

The coloring book line drawings on pages 11–14 can be used as designs for quilt squares.

or

Have students make their own list of things from the story to create each square.

> **Note: It is possible to scan drawings onto cloth to create a quilt. Wash, preshrink, and iron the cloth beforehand.**

1

2

3

4

5

6

7

8

9

10

11

12

Each strip of traditional Seminole patchwork portrays a special symbol. In this fabric, created by seamstress Connie Frank Gowen of the Hollywood reservation, the following symbols are portrayed, from top to bottom:

1. Rain
2. Lightning/Thunder
3. Fire
4. Broken Arrow
5. Man on Horse
6. Bird
7. Four Directions (Medicine Colors)
8. Crawfish
9. Tree
10. Diamondback Rattlesnake
11. Disagree
12. Bones

6 | Song—Forever Florida ©

Words: Mary Lee Powell
Music: Sandy Williams

Flo-ri-da, For-ev-er Flo-ri-da. Glo-ri-ous sun-shine land.

Os-prey waltz-ing on the wind o'er your migh-ty cy-press stands. Great blue her - ron

won't you be our guide? 'Cross the prai - rie, ea - gles at our side.

Flo-ri-da, for-ev-er Flo - ri - da. You're a glo - rious sun-shine land.

Vs. 2   Florida, you're a living legacy with haunting melodies
         Singing rich proud heritage, land so wild and free.
         We hear sweet symphonies of your live oak trees
         Dreams of days gone by, way things ought to be.
         Florida, Forever Florida. You're a land so wild and free.

Vs. 3   Florida, young man dreamin', full of hopes and plans
         Now fore'er part of Florida. Child of this golden land.
         His dreams are risin' with the fog of early morn'
         Living forever in peaceful mists adorned.
         Florida, Forever Florida. Your spirit will live forever.

The inspiration for this song came from a tour at the opening of Forever Florida, a beautiful 3,200-acre wilderness area adjoining a large working cattle ranch in central Florida near Holopaw. A majestic great blue heron became our "guide," flying ahead of our trail coach, as the owners, William and Margaret Broussard, told us of how they have preserved this virgin land in memory of their son, Allen. A poem formed in my spirit. My friend, Sandy Williams, composed the tune for the words. Later we went to Forever Florida and presented our song to the Broussards at a special dinner.

—Lee Powell

7| SUNSHINE STATE STANDARDS

Social Studies Grades 3-5

Strand A:	*Time, Continuity, and Change (History)*	
Standard 1:	*Understands historical chronology and the historical perspective*	
Benchmarks:	SS.A.1.2.1:	*How individuals, ideas, decisions, and events can influence history*
	SS.A.1.2.3:	*Broad categories of time in years, decades, and centuries*

Standard 5:	*United States history from 1880 to the present day*	
Benchmarks:	SS.A.5.2.1:	*Post-Civil War, massive immigration, big business, and mechanized farming transformed American life*
	SS.A.5.2.2:	*Consequences of industrialization and urbanization*
	SS.A.5.2.4:	*Social and cultural transformations of the 1920s and 1930s*

Standard 6:	*History of Florida and its people.*	
Benchmarks:	SS.A.6.2.1:	*Reasons immigrants came to Florida*
	SS.A.6.2.2:	*Influences of geography on history of Florida*
	SS.A.6.2.3:	*Significant individuals, events,*
	SS.A.6.2.4:	*Perspectives of diverse cultural, ethnic, economic groups*
	SS.A.6.2.5:	*How various cultures contributed to Florida*
	SS.A.6.2.6:	*Native American culture in Florida*

Strand B:	*People, Places, and Environments (Geography)*	
Standard 1:	*The world in spatial terms*	
Benchmarks:	SS.B.1.2.1:	*Maps, globes, charts, graphs, etc.*
	SS.B.1.2.2:	*How regions are constructed*

Strand D:	*Production, Distribution, and Consumption (Economics)*	
Standard 1:	*Scarcity*	
Benchmarks:	SS.D.1.2.1:	*Costs and benefits of alternative choices*
	SS.D.1.2.2:	*Scarcity of resources requires choices on many levels*

III|Science

Overview of Integrated Learning Activities

- Illustrate the different types of Florida habitats and list the different types of plants and animals found in each.
- Make triaramas and put them together to create a quadrarama (see p. 55).
- Research plants, animals, and birds that the MacIveys may have seen.
  (e.g., egret, ibis, heron, panther, wild hog, rattlesnakes, muscadine, palmetto, cattails, cypress)
- Cut out pictures from magazines to create a chart for the bulletin board using Florida animal classification:
  > Vertebrates – mammals, amphibians, reptiles, fish, and birds
  > Invertebrates – insects, arachnids, crustaceans, and worms.
- The study of ecology and why recycling is important.
- Bioaccumulation experiment (see p. 53). Students role play a food chain and deduce that the top of the food chain accumulates the most toxins.
- List and study the life cycles of Florida insects. Illustrate the life cycle of a mosquito using the passage from the book (see Excerpt 6, p. 29).
- Send for the kit, *Children are the Future of the Everglades*, prepared by Everglades National Park (see p. 64, Suggested Additional Resources). The kit includes hands-on activities, many reproducible pictures of the animals of the Everglades, and a great video for studying the different Florida habitats. It explains the importance of water conservation and explores the concept that water is the lifeblood of the Everglades.

1 | Researching Florida Plants and Animals

1. Have students skim-read *A Land Remembered* to create a list of the plants and animals that are mentioned. List them on a chart in the classroom. (See example below.)

Plants	Animals
palmetto	herons
cattail	wild hogs
sabal palm	rattle snakes
muscadine	wolves
cypress	deer

2. Then have students choose one plant or animal to research in the library.

3. Have students square-off a plain piece of 8"x10" paper or a piece of notebook paper by folding one corner to the opposite corner.
    Unfold and fold the other corner to the opposite corner.
    Again, unfold and you will have created a criss-cross pattern that forms 4 triangles.

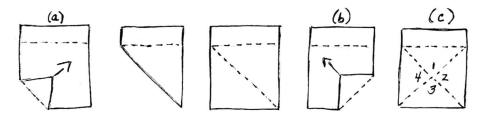

4. Do not cut off the excess. Use it for the title. Write the title on the top (c.).

5. Write a number from 1—4 in each section (c.).

6. Go to the library and find books or websites about your topic (see p. 64, Suggested Additional Resources).

7. Read a paragraph in one of the books or websites.

8. Close the book or put a piece of paper up to cover the screen of your computer and write the details that you remember in your own words in triangle #1.

9. Continue with the technique until you have all four triangles completed with information (in your own words) about your topic.

10. Finally, use this information to write your research paper.

2| Animal Kingdom

The animal kingdom is divided into two main groups: vertebrates (animals with a backbone) and invertebrates (animals without a backbone).

There are five groups of vertebrates:
Mammals – warm-blooded animals in which the females produce milk to feed their young.
Fish – cold-blooded animals that live in water and have scales, fins, and gills.
Birds – warm-blooded creatures with two legs, wings, feathers, and beaks. All birds lay eggs and most can fly.
Reptiles – cold-blooded animals that crawl or creep on short legs. They reproduce by laying eggs.
Amphibians – cold-blooded animals that live in water and breathe with gills when young. As adults, they develop lungs and live on land.

There are many groups of invertebrates. Here are four of the main ones:
Ringed Worms – cold-blooded animals that have a soft body with sections.
Echinoderms – cold-blooded animals that have bodies with rough skin and sharp spines.
Mollusks – cold-blooded animals with a soft body and sometimes a hard shell.
Arthropods – cold-blooded animals with jointed legs.

The small silhouettes of the cow used in the running heads and chapter openings in the student edition of *A Land Remembered* are based on the *Criollo*, a breed of cattle brought to the Americas from Spain. In the 19th century cows of this type ran wild in the Florida scrub. By rounding them up, branding them, and driving them to market, Tobias MacIvey began his life as a successful cattleman.

Florida is still a cattle state and several ranches offer opportunities to glimpse this still thriving way of life. Many tours include adjacent wilderness areas with unspoiled pinewoods, marshes, and abundant native birds and wildlife.

Forever Florida
4755 N. Kenansville Road, St. Cloud, FL 34755
phone: (888) 957-9794 or
(866) 85-4-EVER (3837)
e-mail: Foreverflorida@impinet.net
website: www.foreverflorida.com
    www.floridaeco-safaris.com
4,500 acres. Wilderness exploration, hiking trails, horseback rides, bicycle rentals. Also visit nearby Crescent J Ranch.

Babcock Wilderness Adventures
8000 State Road 31, Punta Gorda, FL 33982
phone: (800) 500-5583
e-mail: adventure@babcockwilderness.com
website: www.babcockwilderness.com
90,000-acre Crescent B Ranch. Swamp buggy tours, 3-hour bike tours, museum and natural history exhibits, educational programs. All tours must be prebooked.

FLORIDA ANIMALS

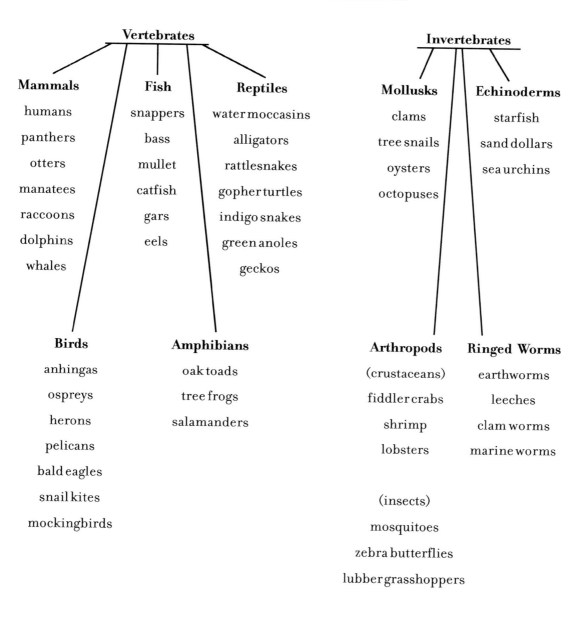

Vertebrates

Mammals
humans
panthers
otters
manatees
raccoons
dolphins
whales

Fish
snappers
bass
mullet
catfish
gars
eels

Reptiles
water moccasins
alligators
rattlesnakes
gopher turtles
indigo snakes
green anoles
geckos

Invertebrates

Mollusks
clams
tree snails
oysters
octopuses

Echinoderms
starfish
sand dollars
sea urchins

Birds
anhingas
ospreys
herons
pelicans
bald eagles
snail kites
mockingbirds

Amphibians
oak toads
tree frogs
salamanders

Arthropods
(crustaceans)
fiddler crabs
shrimp
lobsters

(insects)
mosquitoes
zebra butterflies
lubber grasshoppers

(arachnids)
banana spiders
brown recluse spiders

Ringed Worms
earthworms
leeches
clam worms
marine worms

3 | The Study of Ecology

This is an outline that may be used as a guide for your study of Ecology.

I.   An Introduction to Environmental Learning
     A.   Everything in our world is connected
     B.   Making a difference

II. Ecosystems and Habitats
     A.   Food chains
     B.   Food webs

III. Our Natural Resources
     A.   Trees
     B.   Water
     C.   Soil

IV. Threatened and Endangered Species
     A.   Bioaccumulation (see directions for game on next page)
     B.   Extinct species
     C.   Species making a comeback
     D.   Exotics - why are they bad?

V.   Environmental Concerns
     A.   Air pollution
     B.   Acid rain
     C.   The ozone layer
     D.   Water pollution
     E.   Water conservation
     F.   Our oceans
     G.   Solid waste and litter
     H.   Recycling

VI. Energy Conservation
     A.   Why is it important?
     B.   What can we do?

*Note: A great book for students to use is *The Young Naturalist's Guide to Florida*, by Peggy Sias Lantz and Wendy A. Hale, Pineapple Press, 1994.

4 | Bioaccumulation Activity

Have students write these terms and illustrate them before introducing the outside activity:

1. **Interrelationships**: organisms interacting with each other in their environment.
2. **Ecology**: the study of the interrelationships of all living and non-living things.
3. **Adaptation**: special characteristics that make an organism more suited to its environment.
4. **Food chain**: sequence of organisms, starting with green plants, in which each is food for higher and more complex organisms.
5. **Food web**: the many connected food chains by which organisms of a community obtain their energy.

What is bioaccumulation, and how does it affect Florida wildlife?

This activity was designed in order to study the impact of bioaccumulation on organisms at different levels of a food chain.

Remind students that light energy is converted by plants into food energy, which is then transferred to an animal when the plant is eaten. The energy is passed up each level of the food chain when animals eat other animals.

Materials:

- Role-playing animal tags
- permanent marker
- red food coloring
- popcorn
- clear plastic cups
- safety pins
- spray bottle

After popping the popcorn, color about one third of the pieces with red food coloring by putting colored water in a spray bottle. Be careful not to soak the popcorn, just lightly spray it. The red popcorn will represent plants that have been contaminated with bioaccumulating toxins.

The Game:

List the following organisms on the board:

—water plants
—small fish
—large fish
—brown pelicans

Explain that for this activity, the popcorn represents the plants in the food chain. Students will be assuming the roles of the small fish, large fish, and brown pelicans in a food chain. Distribute animal tags and pin one tag on each student's back.

> **Note: For a class of 26-35 students, plan on 2-3 brown pelicans, 6-9 large fish, and 18-23 small fish.**

Distribute marked cups to students, and explain that the cups represent the stomachs of the animals. During the game, the small fish must try to find enough food to fill their cups one-third full; the large fish must find enough food to fill their cups two-thirds full; and the brown pelicans must gather enough food to fill their cups nearly all the way.

Small fish can only collect popcorn directly from the ground. The only way the large fish can collect popcorn they need is to tag a small fish and take the contents of its stomach. The only way a brown pelican can collect the popcorn it needs is to tag a large fish and take the contents of its stomach. Start the small fish with a 15-second head start, then the large fish 15 seconds before the brown pelicans.

The only way the small and large fish can survive is if they collect enough food to fill their stomachs before they are tagged by an animal above them in the food chain. The only way the brown pelicans can survive is if they collect enough food to fill their stomachs before the game is over.

When animals collect enough food to fill their stomachs, they should run to the edge of the playing area and wait for the game to end. If an animal is tagged by a predator higher up in the food chain before its stomach is full, the tagged animal must give the predator all of the food in its stomach and go to the edge of the playing field and die. The game will be over when all animals have died or have obtained all the food they need.

After the Game:
Students count the number of colored and uncolored pieces of popcorn and construct a class data table summarizing each student's results. Animals that died before they obtained enough food to survive will record 0 for all three columns.

Animal type	No. of popcorn pieces collected	No. of uncolored popcorn pieces	No. of red popcorn pieces

Finally, introduce the term **bioaccumulation as the accumulation of toxic substances in successive layers of a food chain.** Explain that the red pieces of popcorn collected during the class activity represent units of toxic food items.

Tell students that the lethal dose of toxin for small fish was 5 units, the lethal dose for large fish was 7 units, and the lethal dose for brown pelicans was 10 units. Also explain that if pelicans accumulated more than 8 units of toxic food, they would be unable to reproduce because the eggshells would be too thin and would break before the baby pelicans could hatch.

Conclude the lesson by asking students what can be done to reduce the problems caused by toxic substances in Florida's environment.

5 | Creating Triaramas and Quadraramas

If you have ever made a diorama using a shoebox, you will understand the concept of triaramas. They are a three-dimensional way for students to display what they have learned. Four triaramas can be glued together to form a quadrarama.

1. Start with construction paper that has been squared off. Fold the top right corner of the square down to the lower left corner. Repeat with the opposite corners.
2. Open and cut one fold line to the center of the square.
3. Draw a background scene on half the square as shown.
4. Overlap the two bottom triangles and glue. Add stand-up parts to complete the triarama.

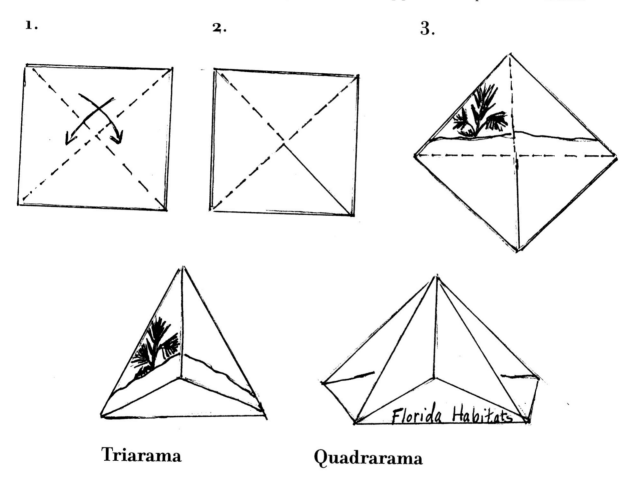

1.   **2.**   **3.**

Triarama   **Quadrarama**

These can be used for Language Arts, Science, or Social Studies Activities.

Language Arts   Make a *triarama* representing the setting and characters of the story. On a *quadrarama*, show and write about the sequence of important events in a story.

Social Studies   Use a triarama to show your knowledge of people, places, and events. Write about what you have learned on the back.

Science   Illustrate how everything in our world is connected or interrelated using food webs. Depict how litter is harmful to animals and show solutions to the problem. Create quadraramas of the different Florida habitats.

6 | SUNSHINE STATE STANDARDS

Science Grades 3-5

Strand A:	*Matter*
Standard 2	*Interaction of matter and energy.*
Benchmark:	*SC.B.2.2.2: Costs and risks of using nonrenewable energy*
Strand D:	*Processes that Shape the Earth*
Standard 2:	*Protection of the natural systems on Earth.*
Benchmark:	*SC.D.2.2.1: Reusing, recycling, and reducing*
Strand G:	*Environment*
Standard 1:	*Interdependent, cyclic nature of living things in the environment.*
Benchmarks:	*SC.G.1.2.1: Interaction of plants and animals*
	SC.G.1.2.2: Adapting to the environment
	SC.G.1.2.4: Recycling matter
	SC.G.1.2.5: Transfer of energy
	SC.G.1.2.6: New organisms are produced from dead organisms
	SC.G.1.2.7: Population densities in an ecosystem
Standard 2:	*Limited natural resources.*
Benchmarks:	*SC.G.2.2.1: Passing adaptations to offspring*
	SC.G.2.2.3: Habitat changes
Strand H:	*Nature of Science*
Standard 2:	*Patterns of natural events*
Benchmark:	*SC.H.2.2.1: Natural events are often predictable and logical*
Standard 3:	*Science, technology, and society are interwoven and interdependent.*
Benchmarks:	*S.C.H.3.2.1: Tools to solve problems*
	S.C.H.3.2.3: Effects of building something new
	S.C.H.3.2.4: Solving problems, making decisions, and forming new ideas

Appendix

Summary of Integrated Learning Activities for the Study of Florida History,
Coordinated with the Foxfire Core Practices

Core Practice #1: The work teachers and learners do together is infused from the beginning with learner choice, design, and revision. The central focus of the work grows out of learners' interests and concerns. **Most problems that arise during classroom activity are solved in collaboration with learners, and learners are supported in the development of their ability to solve problems and accept responsibility.**

1. Begin with a planning session. Use the overview of *A Land Remembered*. Explain that it will be used to enhance your study of Florida history. Help students to create a picture in their mind of what the wilderness area of Florida was like during the Civil War era. Do a walk back in time using pictures, videos, and field trips. What was central Florida like before the influx of tourism?

2. Discuss the importance of preserving the heritage and protecting the environment. Point out that the book explores the key issues of what happens when we interfere with the environment and that change is not always for the better. "Everything in our World is Connected" could be a central theme.

3. Show pictures of the Everglades and point out the area on a map of Florida. Explain that it was once considered to be just a swamp that needed to be dried up so that Miami could expand. Read to students the first section of the book, *The Everglades* by Marjory Stoneman Douglas that captures the essence of what it was once like before man interfered.

4. Record students' concerns on chart paper and use the chart during future planning sessions. Be open and allow students to be creative.

Core Practice #2: The role of the teacher is that of facilitator and collaborator: **Teachers are responsible for assessing and attending to learners' developmental needs, providing guidance, identifying academic givens, monitoring each learner's academic and social growth, and leading each into new areas of understanding and competence.**

1. Create two different charts using student input. Good Teacher / Good Student
    Ask students what it takes to be a good teacher and a good student. Record their answers for each to create the individual charts.

2. Explain your role as a facilitator and how you will help each student learn the academic givens (Sunshine State Standards, see pp. 38, 47, and 56).

3. Get students involved in solving the problems.

Core Practice #3: The academic integrity of the work teachers and learners do together is clear. **Mandated skills and learning expectations are identified to the class. Through collaborative planning and implementation, students engage and accomplish the mandates. In addition, activities assist learners in discovering the value and potential of the curriculum and its connections to other disciplines.**

1. Explain to the students what the state standards are. Go over the grade level expectations and rewrite them in their own words.
2. Post these as your givens that must be covered and refer to them throughout your study of Florida history. Have students check off the givens that are covered throughout the study.

Core Practice #4: The work is characterized by active learning. **Learners are thoughtfully engaged in the learning process, posing and solving problems, making meaning, producing products, and building understandings. Because learners engaged in these kinds of activities are risk takers operating on the edge of their competence, the classroom environment provides an atmosphere of trust where the consequence of a mistake is the opportunity for further learning.**

1. Each student must choose one area of Florida history to research and present to the class or a wider audience.
2. Widen the audience and create a Florida Fair where all projects are displayed for the whole school to view. Some examples of what we have done to widen the audience are:
    -   working with students to restore a depression era cannery into a museum of Florida history.
    -   having other classes in the district come to the museum on field trips to learn about Florida history from our student guides.
    -   putting on an annual Frolic that creates a walk back in time for the whole community. The Frolic includes booths and demonstrations of the old time crafts and traditions as well as the traditional menu of wild hog, swamp cabbage, black-eyed peas, cornbread, collard greens, and sweet potatoes.
    -   working in the garden at the cannery and researching ways to improve the harvest.
3. Students work in cooperative groups to produce quality work. They must be given time to collaborate and build understanding.

Core Practice #5: Peer teaching, small group work, and teamwork are all consistent features of classroom activities. **Every learner is not only included, but also needed, and, in the end, each can identify her or his specific stamp upon the effort.**

1. Each student must be actively involved in the group and take ownership of their part in the whole project, saying, "I did that" with pride and conviction.

Core Practice #6: Connections between the classroom work, the surrounding communities, and the world beyond community are clear. **Course content is connected to the community in which the learners live. Learners' work will "bring home" larger issues by identifying attitudes about and illustrations and implications of those issues in their home communities.**

1. Find a community connection. Did your students come up with something during the planning sessions that they were concerned about (i.e., recycling, pollution, more and more building—less and less natural environment)? Ask them to think of ways they can make a difference.
2. Identify the issues. Record ideas and create a community project.

Core Practice #7: There is an audience beyond the teacher for learner work. **It may be another individual, or a small group, or the community, but it is an audience the learners want to serve or engage. The audience, in turn, affirms the work is important, needed, and worth doing.**

1. The community project you create will be enjoyed by the ultimate audience.
2. This should be a project beyond the classroom and the teacher—to reach an audience the students want to engage.

Core Practice #8: New activities spiral gracefully out of the old, incorporating lessons learned from past experiences, building on skills and understandings that can now be amplified. **Rather than completion of a study being regarded as the conclusion of a series of activities, it is regarded as the starting point for a new series.**

1. Your project will continually spiral. Ask, "Where do we go from here?" New ideas will spiral from the old.

2. Examples: We created a Frolic to share our need to preserve the heritage with the whole community; consequently we went on a cattle drive because of the cow camp at the Frolic.
    -   We painted murals on the walls and a map of Florida on the floor in the Cannery Annex because of our study of Florida history.
    -   We created a video of our project because of the need to do a video exchange with the Miccosukee Indians in the Everglades.

Core Practice #9: Imagination and creativity are encouraged in the completion of learning activities. **It is the learners' freedom to express and explore, to observe and investigate, and to discover that are the basis for aesthetic experiences. These experiences provide a sense of enjoyment and satisfaction and lead to deeper understanding and an internal thirst for knowledge.**

1. Help students to create high quality work. The satisfaction of a job well done is the ultimate aesthetic experience.

2. Examples of aesthetics: Essays, Brochures, Video, Write and sing songs, Grow vegetables in the Cannery garden, The marketplace at the Frolic, Paint murals, Present the play *A Land Remembered*, Florida history projects and posters.

Core Practice #10: Reflection is an essential activity that takes place at key points throughout the work. **Teachers and learners engage in conscious and thoughtful consideration of the work and the process. It is this reflective activity that evokes insight and gives rise to revisions and refinement.**

-   Have students keep a journal and write daily or weekly reflections of what they are doing. Honest evaluation is encouraged and not condemned. Students need to ask: What are we doing to achieve our goals? What have we done well and what can we do better?

Core Practice #11: The work teachers and learners do together includes rigorous, ongoing assessment and evaluation. **Teachers and learners employ a variety of strategies to demonstrate their mastery of teaching and learning objectives.**

-   Create rubrics (see example) for ongoing assessment throughout your Florida history study. Connect evaluations with the Sunshine State Standards.

Permission to use the Core Practices was granted by The Foxfire Fund, Inc., P.O. Box 541, Mountain City, GA30562-0541.

Glossary—Volume 1

adz (adze) – an axlike tool with an arching blade used for dressing wood

allapattah – Seminole for alligator

auger – a tool for boring holes in wood or earth

auger bit – a bit with a blade like that of an auger

bay head – a low, swampy place with bay trees growing thick—very hard to go through—only thing worse is a marsh

black jacks – scrub oaks

boar – a wild hog with a hairy coat and a long snout. Also, an uncastrated hog.

brackish – water that is part salt water

broad axe – an ax with a broad blade used as a weapon or for cutting timber

bushwhacker – someone who attacks from ambush, or, one who is accustomed to beating or cutting his way through bushes

cabbage palm – type of palm tree having an edible heart

canter – smooth, easy pace like a moderate gallop

carcass – the dead body of an animal

chickee hut – an open-air platform raised off the ground with no walls and a thatched roof. Commonly used by the Seminole Indians.

cocoplum bush – a tree which yields an edible fruit like a plum, it is native to tropical America

collard – a kind of kale whose coarse leaves are born in tufts—cooked, eaten, and called collard green

commercial – having to do with stores, office buildings, etc.

conquistador – any one of the Spanish conquerors of South or Central America in the 16th century

corral – a pen or enclosure for cattle

cracklins – meat skin fried very crispy

cure meat – to flavor and preserve it

cypress – any of a large group of cone-bearing trees of the pine family native to North America, Europe, and Asia

cypress stand or head – an area where most of the trees are cypress

drawing knife (or draw knife) – a knife with a handle at each end, usually at right angles to the blade

dredge – a device consisting of a net attached to a frame, dragged along the bottom of a river or bay

drover – one who drives cattle or sheep to market

dutch oven – a cast-iron cooking utensil

entrails – the inner organs of men or animals

ferry – to carry or transport something across a river or water by boat

fetch – to go after things and bring them back

froe – a wedge-shaped cleaving tool with a handle set into the blade at right angles to the back

gibberish – rapid, inarticulate talk—unintelligible chatter

hammock – a piece of rich land with hardwood trees growing on it

hardwood – any tough, heavy timber with a compact texture

high hammock – an area of mostly live oaks, red cedars, slash pine, hickories, magnolias, and cabbage palms

hitching rail – a place to harness or attach a horse to a vehicle, or a pole used to tie animals to

homestead – a home—the seat of a family—including the land, house, and outbuildings

irrigate – to bring water to

koonti flour – made from root of sago palm, commonly used by the Seminole Indians lean-to – a roof with a single slope, its upper edge abutting a wall or building

low hammock – an area of mostly sweet bay, red bay, black gum, sweet gum, some magnolias, cabbages, and palms

mangrove – any of several coastal or aquatic tropical trees or shrubs that form large colonies in swamps

manure – natural animal fertilizers

Marshtackie – a horse—offspring of those left behind by Spanish soldiers—very small and runty, but very strong

mine – a large excavation in the earth to extract metallic ores, coal, precious stones, salt, or certain other minerals

musket – a smoothbore, long-handled firearm used especially by infantry soldiers before the invention of the rifle

Okeechobee – a lake in south Florida

palmetto – one of several species of palm trees growing in the West Indies and in the southern part of the United States

Pay-Hay-Okee – the great marsh—the river of grass—made of saw grass dotted with small island hammocks

pewter – an alloy of tin with lead, brass, or copper. It takes on a grayish, silvery color when polished

phosphate – a salt of phosphoric acid containing PO_4

pickerelweed – a sprawling evergreen perennial with heart-shaped leaves, growing to 4 feet tall

plumes – feathers

poke greens – an edible weed cooked and eaten as a vegetable

predators – plunderers or robbers (also bears, panthers, or wolves)

pukin' – vomiting

quilting bee – a social gathering of women at which they sew quilts

savannah – an extensive open plain in a tropical region of seasonal rains, destitute of trees and covered with grass

saw grass – a marsh grass having linear leaves with sharp, saw-toothed edges

scalded hog – butchered hog placed in pot of boiling water, then the hide scraped to remove hair and bristles

scrawny – lean, thin, scraggy, scrubby

scrub – short, stunted tree or bush, or shrubs growing thickly together

scrub palmettos – saw palmettos—stems will cut dogs and people passing through them

needle palmettos – found in the flatwoods on the edge of the hammock

sharecropper – a tenant farmer who obtains land, a house, tools, and seeds for farming on credit from a landowner

shinny – to climb by using the shins for gripping

sidewheel steamer – a steamboat having a paddle wheel on each side

slough – a place of deep mud or mire—a swamp, bog, or marsh

smokehouse – where the meat was smoked and cured

"sommers" – somewhere

Spanish bayonets – a species of Yucca growing in deserts having sword-shaped, sharp, pointed, rigid leaves

stern-wheeler – a steam vessel propelled by a single paddle wheel at the back

swamp cabbage – the heart or center of the cabbage palm removed and cooked as a side dish

Timucuan – native tribesman

titi – a small evergreen tree or shrub with fragrant white or pinkish flowers, found in swamps in the southern United States

turban – any of various styles of headdress worn by men in the middle east and orient

turkey oaks – scrub oaks

tusk – a long, pointed tooth—usually one of a pair—projecting outside the mouth and used for defense and digging

udder – a mammary gland, especially one that is large and pendulous with two or more teats, as in cows

varmints – animals or bugs considered to be pests

"vittles" – what food was commonly called

whiskey still – an apparatus used for distilling liquids, especially alcoholic liquors

yellowhammer – a type of cow

Glossary – Volume 2

bandana – a large, colored handkerchief

barn raising – a community effort to quickly build a barn

blizzard – a violent snowstorm

bowler hats – small rounded hats

brogan shoes – heavy work shoes

buckboard – a long, flat wagon

bushwhack – to be caught off guard

cantankerous – grumpy, moody, of ill temperament

canter – a fast, three-beat gait of the horse

carcasses – dead bodies (in this case, cattle)

cattle lowing – mooing

chandelier – fancy lighting fixture

chickees – shelters built by Florida's Native Americans—open-air platforms raised off the ground with thatched roofs and no walls

clan – family

coal oil lamp – an oil-burning lamp used for light (prior to electricity)

contrasting – comparing similar things

coontie bread – bread made from flour produced from the roots of the Sago palm

cranked the car – cars used to be started with a crank on the front of the car

"deef" – deaf, unable to hear

deformed – misshapen

devastated – completely overwhelmed with grief

dike – a barrier put around a body of water to prevent flooding

down – soft feathers from geese

drenching – a complete soaking

dressed cows – ready to eat

drought – time of little or no rain

eerie – spooky

egret plumes – feathers from an egret

encounter – to come across, to meet

endure – to suffer hardships without giving in

eye of the hurricane – the center of the storm—a very still, quiet time during a hurricane

fate – your destiny, where life takes you

financial boom – profitable time

flanks – sides

fodder – livestock feed

fury – violent anger

gaily – happily

gloom – darkness

gnarled – twisted, full of knots

gorging – eating too much

gunslingers – men that carried guns

hammock – a dry area that supports hardwood trees such as oak, pines, or cedars

heed – to take advice

hightail it – to leave quickly

hog scrapin' – scraping the hide of a hog

hog slop – food for hogs

horrified – to cause or feel horror

hover – to linger close by

huckleberries – large, sweet berries similar to blueberries

humdinger – amazing

hurl – to throw

isolation – separation from others

itinerant preacher – traveling minister of the church

Julia Tuttle – founder of Miami

knead – to work dough by pressing and squeezing

knickerbockers – knee-length men's trousers

lanky – tall and slender

lard – melted hog fat

lobby – main entrance

lumber – wood used for building things

malaria – a disease caused by mosquitoes

mangled – damaged, twisted

mangrove – coastal trees that grow in salt or brackish water

mare – female horse

mark-brand – a mark placed on cattle to prove ownership

marsh – low, wet swamp

muck – fertile ground left after swamps are drained

nostrils – external openings of the nose

outhouse hole – outdoor toilet

palmetto clump – a grouping of saw palmetto plants

parasols – fashionable umbrellas used primarily for sun protection

pastries – sweet baked goods

pay last respects – to attend a funeral

Pay-Hay-Okee – Seminole Indian word for the Everglades meaning "river of grass"

planks – heavy, thick boards

plunder – to rob

plunge – to drive into

podium degree – college degree given to someone who did not earn it

poinciana tree – a small, sub-tropical tree with red or yellow flowers

poinsettia – small shrub with red leaves at the top—leaves resemble flowers

poultice – hot, soft mass applied to a sore spot on the body

prediction – a foretelling

prism – triangular piece of crystal or glass that refracts light into rainbow colors

procession – a number of people or things moving forward

raid – a sudden, unexpected attack

rampant – running wild

ramrod straight – very erect and straight

rations – small portions of food

recruits – hired help

reservation – a guaranteed spot at a hotel or restaurant

roasting spit – a device used over an open fire that slowly turns a hog or cow while cooking

Royal Poinciana Hotel – luxury hotel

saliva – the watery fluid secreted by glands in the mouth

scurrying – running away

second phase – the second and more violent part of a hurricane after the eye passes over

slaughter – the killing of animals for food

sleet – frozen or partly frozen rain

slough – wet, swampy area

slush – partially melted ice and snow

squatters – people who live on property they do not own

stallion – male horse

stirrups – foot rings attached by straps to a saddle

stockpiling – storing supplies for lean times

stoked the fire – stirred, added more fuel

suite – several rooms in a hotel grouped together as a unit

surplus – more than what is needed

swamp cabbage – the center of the cabbage palm, boiled and eaten

sweet gum – A North American tree with lobbed leaves and hard wood

Thomas Edison – inventor of the incandescent light bulb

thunderhead – storm clouds

time capsule – a container that can be opened at a later time, to preserve a time in history

trudging – moving slowly with difficulty

twilight – the time of day when it is not quite light or dark

veranda – covered porch

wheeled about – turned quickly

whiskey into wound – antiseptic

whiskey still – a distillery to make whiskey

wicker – woven sticks made into furnishings

Suggested Additional Resources

Books:

African Americans in Florida, by Maxine D. Jones and Kevin M. McCarthy, Pineapple Press, Inc., 1993.

Florida Cattle Ranch, by Alto Adams and Lee Gramling Jr., Pineapple Press, Inc., 1998.

Legends of the Seminoles, by Betty Mae Jumper with Peter Gallagher, Pineapple Press, Inc., 1994.

Native Americans in Florida, by Kevin M. McCarthy, Pineapple Press, Inc., 1999.

The Everglades: River of Grass, by Marjory Stoneman Douglas, 50th Anniversary Edition, Pineapple Press, Inc., 1997.

The Young Naturalist's Guide to Florida, by Peggy Sias Lantz and Wendy A. Hale, Pineapple Press, Inc., 1994.

Who Really Killed Cock-Robin? by Jean Craighead George. This is an ecological mystery that refers to bioaccumulation.

Newspapers:

Florida Studies Weekly, Published by States Studies Weekly, Inc., P.O. Box 264, American Fork, UT 84003. This is a weekly newspaper written on a 4th-5th grade reading level that follows a timeline of Florida history. http://studiesweekly.com

Earth Preservers, The environmental newspaper for kids, Earth Preservers, Inc., P.O. Box 6, Westfield, NJ 07091. http://www.earthpreservers.com

Kit:

Children Are the Future of the Everglades, a curriculum for 4th grade teachers, is available by mail from the Everglades Association, 40001 State Road 9336, Homestead, FL 33034 or by phone at (305)247-1216. This kit contains hands-on activities for children to explore the importance of water conservation. The video included in the kit is an excellent tool to use for the study of Florida habitats.

CDs:

Echoes of Nature. Kim Wilson. Delta Music, Inc., Santa Monica, CA 90404. 1993. This CD contains the natural sounds of a tropical wilderness area. Available through Amazon.com

CD ROMs:

Energy and Environmental Issues. An interactive CD-ROM, 1997. Florida State University, C220 University Center, Tallahassee, FL 32306-4016. Grant #DE-FG44-77Cs-60210. http://eea.freac.fsu.edu. (Click on materials)

CLASP. Children's Language Arts & Science Project. Storybook CD-ROM, Interactive activities about taking care of the environment. Students can choose English or Spanish. Energy & Environmental Alliance, Florida State University, UCC2200, Tallahassee, FL 32306-2641. http://eea.freac.fsu.edu. (Click on materials)

Best Websites:

http://www.floridahistory.org
http://dhr.dos.state.fl.us/ (Click on kids page)
Check out Florida history and environmental websites for information and lesson plans

CPSIA information can be obtained at www.ICGtesting.com
Printed in the USA
270377BV00002B/3/P